A lone rider and his mystery horse leapt across scary ravines, galloped through giant prickly cacti, passed rocks speckled with gold dust and carved with the faces of important people.

"He's a-comin'!" cried the rider, Wild West Bob, who sped into town. "He's a-comin' right behind me!"

"Our hero!" gasped the locals, as they watched Mucky Muck, the most famous adventurer in the West, empty a prisoner from his dumper. Thump!

The air grew poisonous as the masked prisoner let out a gigantic burp.

"Yep," said Wild West Bob, coughing at the terrible smell, "there's no mistakin' Stinky Spud, the most wanted scarecrow in the West."

"Good work!" cried Sheriff Bentley, who dropped a sack of gleaming gold into Mucky Muck's digger before taking the villain off to jail.

"Yeehah!" exclaimed the real Muck, who had been daydreaming on the train. "Wow! I am going to have brilliant adventures on our Wild West holiday."

The real Bob nodded and looked out of the train window at the dusty desert all around. "A trip to the Wild West is amazing, isn't it."

"Sure is," said Muck, "'cos I was built to be wild!"

"Yes indeedy," Bob chuckled, and he began to sing a jolly song about going on a cowboy holiday and doing no more building for a week or two.

The train gave a happy hoot as it drew closer to its holiday destination.

A battered pick-up truck called Jackaroo was there to meet Bob, Wendy and the machine team, at Cactus Creek station.

"Welcome to the Wild West, folks!" said Jackaroo. "Climb aboard."

"Thanks for the ride," said Bob. "Muck can't wait to see what adventures you've got planned for him!"

"You see," Muck explained seriously, "I was built to be wild."

Jackaroo hooted with laughter. "Oh there'll be plenty of wild for you at the Double R Ranch!"

"What a fantastic place!" sighed Wendy as they looked across the valley and desert, to Cactus Creek and the ranch.

"Howdy folks!" called a woman wearing a big cowboy hat. "I'm Rio Rogers and this here's my horse Dollar. Pleased to meet y'all."

Dollar whinnied, and everyone said hello.

Jackaroo explained that Cactus Creek used to be a gold mining town. When the gold ran out, all the gold hunters left town. "So that left me, Rio, Dollar, and hundreds of…"

"Cacti!" laughed Wendy. "We noticed."

The Double R Ranch had seen better days, and Bob couldn't resist trying to fix the broken sign. Wendy gently reminded him: "No more fixing for a week or two!"

"You're right," Bob said, turning to see a cow trying to escape from the ranch.

"That's my cow, Brandy," laughed Rio as she skilfully caught the cow with her lasso.

"I bet you've had loads of adventures out here," sighed Muck, as Jackaroo helped pitch their tents for the night.

"Yep-diddle," Jackaroo boasted, "we've seen stuff that'd make yer paint rust!"

Round the blazing campfire Rio told the amazing story of her fight with a snake as big as a barn, which she won by throwing the snake right round the world!

Muck gasped, and said that more than anything he wanted people to tell campfire stories about him.

"I'm not just a dumper truck you know – I was built to be wild!"

Next morning it was time for a cowboy lesson with Rio.

"Buffalo Bob," she called. "See if you can lasso Brandy."

But Bob only managed to lasso himself before falling in the water trough.

When Bob tried to ride Rio's horse Dollar, he shot away at great speed, and just before falling off Bob cried: "I can't find the brakes!"

Rio said that he should do what her great, great Grandaddy always advised – get straight back on again.

"Ooohh," chuckled Bob. "I think I have a lot to learn."

"Rio's great, great Grandaddy was the first to strike gold in Cactus Creek," Jackaroo explained. "He started a gold rush. Hey, Muck! I'll show you and Spud the old mine."

"An adventure at last," thought Muck. But when they arrived at the mine the entrance was blocked.

"Closed down long ago," said Jackaroo. "Tooooo dangerous."

Muck was just wondering how to get into the gold mine when Brandy the cow clattered past again.

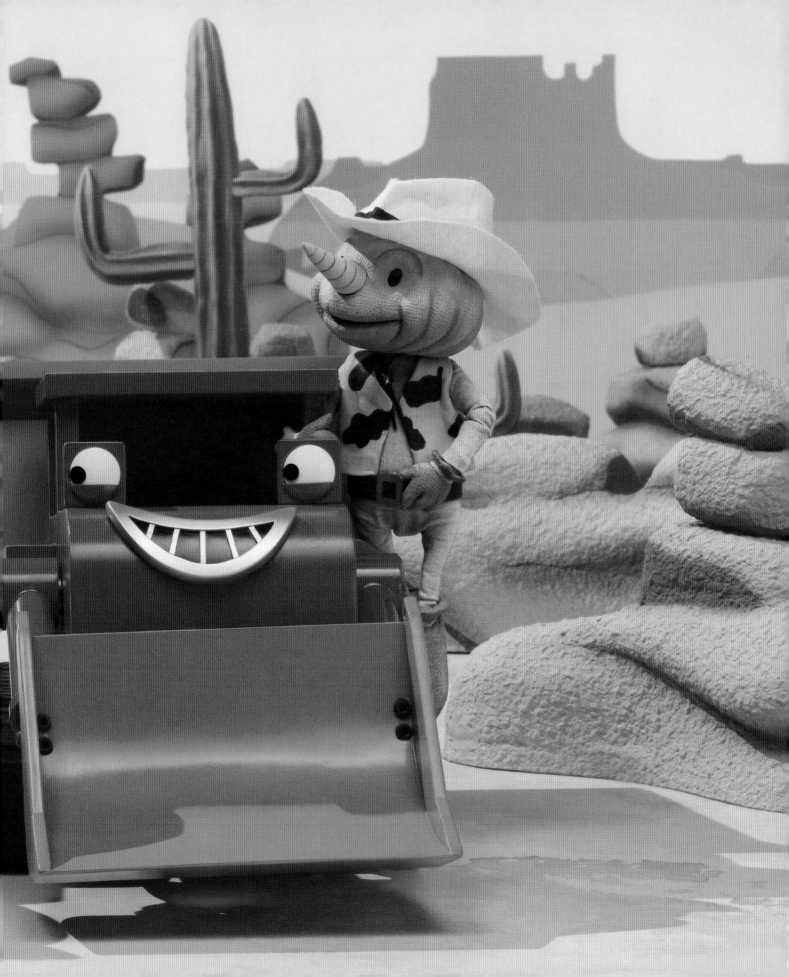

During the cow-catching chaos that followed as Jackaroo, Muck and Spud tried to stop Brandy running off, Muck smashed into the beautiful old Cactus Creek saloon. He stared in disbelief as the building collapsed around him.

"Oh, no! What have I done?" cried Muck, as the rest of the old town collapsed like a row of falling dominoes. There was rubble and dust everywhere.

"Hot diggety dawg!" moaned Jackaroo. "That's one big mess!" They saw a group of riders approaching on the horizon.

"This old town means everything to me," Rio was telling Bob and Wendy. Then she did a double-take. "Oh no! My great, great Grandaddy's town's in ruins!"

Muck told Rio he was very sorry. Rio was kind. She said it was OK because she knew Muck was only trying to help. Bob inspected the support posts of the saloon.

"Actually," he said, "this wood is rotten."

Rio looked sad. "I'm a-runnin' my cowboy adventure holidays to fix up the place," she said, "but Cactus Creek is in a worse state than I realised."

"Don't worry," said Bob. "What you're about to find out is that I have the best building team in the whole world."

"Can we fix it?" called Scoop.

"Yes we can!" replied Bob and the gang.

Rio was so happy. "Why, y'all are the nicest folks I ever did meet. Thank you so much."

Bob and Wendy used pick-axes to remove the rotten wood, then cut timber for a new frame. In no time, four new support posts were set into concrete. Scoop filled his front digger time and again, and Muck helped to carry the dirt away.

"Good work, team!" Bob praised.

Around the campfire that night Spud burped on his beans just like the villainous Stinky Spud in Muck's daydream on the journey to Cactus Creek.

Coyotes wailed in the distance as Rio sang of her great, great Grandaddy the day he scooped some drinking water in his hat and saw little nuggets of gold glinting at the bottom.

"Gold fever…" Rio sang. "Hundreds of folk flocking for gold - their own clutch o' gold… great, great Grandaddy, legend is, you hid yer treasure for us to find… hidden gold, gold fever."

"Wow," thought Muck before going to sleep. "I wouldn't mind an adventure like that. I was built to be wild!"

Next morning, bright and early as the sun was rising, Bob called for his team to get building.

"Aw," moaned Muck. "I want an adventure, not work!"

Rio laughed, and invited Muck and Spud to travel with her for supplies. She warned everyone to take it nice and slow across a rickety bridge, but when heavy Jackaroo and Muck trundled on together the ropes began to fray...

"Waargh!" wailed Muck, just making it to the other side.

And then the ropes began to snap and unravel...

"Aarrrrrgh!" squealed Spud, who was still on the bridge.

Wheeeeeeeeeeeee! the bridge plunged down the sheer sides of the creek, taking poor Spud with it. Muck called out for his friend. Luckily, Spud was still hanging on.

Rio quick as a flash lassoed him, making it easy for Muck to pull Spud up using the rope.

"Phew!" Spud panted. "That was er – a bit of a scary adventure."

As they headed back with sheets of glass, roofing felt, wood and paint for repairing Cactus Creek, Muck wondered when it would be his turn for excitement.

Back at Cactus Creek, Rio, Jackaroo, Muck and Spud found Bob directing Lofty to lift up a side panel and Scoop to push. Bob and Wendy then moved in with drills to fix it in place.

"Jumpin' Jackrabbits!" said Jackaroo, amazed to see how much progress they had made.

Spud told Bob and Wendy about the scary broken bridge, and Bob was relieved everyone was safe.

Muck was given the job of clearing out the old barn.

"At this rate, we'll be on our way home before I squeeze in a single Wild West adventure!" sighed Muck to himself.

When the team stopped for lunch, Rio started telling a tale about sharing a tree with a grizzly bear and being chased for two whole days by a swarm of vicious bees. Muck listened in amazement, dreaming of his own Wild West adventures.

Spud decided to go off on his own and do a bit of exploring. He went in to the old barn to take a look round. He instantly noticed a rock shaped like the 'R' of the Rogers family. When he pushed it hard, the ground opened up in front of his eyes!

Spud called out to Muck, "This is a real adventure – not a silly old story."

But Muck didn't hear him. He was too busy listening to another Rio Wild West adventure.

"Oh, well," said Spud to himself. "I'll just have a quick look in here and then go and get Muck."

Spud found an old miner's lamp and stepped through the hole into the dark tunnel…

"Uh-oh! It's pretty gloomy down here," said Spud.

He climbed into one of the old railway carts that used to carry the gold-speckled rocks to the surface of Cactus Creek.

"I wonder what this lever does?" Spud said to himself, as he pulled on a lever on the cart. "Waaaaaaarrgh! Muck, help me!" cried Spud loudly, as the cart shot forwards down a rickety old track.

Muck heard Spud's call for help and rolled over to the barn. Seeing the mysterious hole in the floor, he nervously rolled inside. Underground, Muck saw Spud zooming off into the gloom. He found another cart, got in and released the brake. He zoomed into the dark after Spud. Finally, Spud and Muck both came to a bumpy halt at the end of the track.

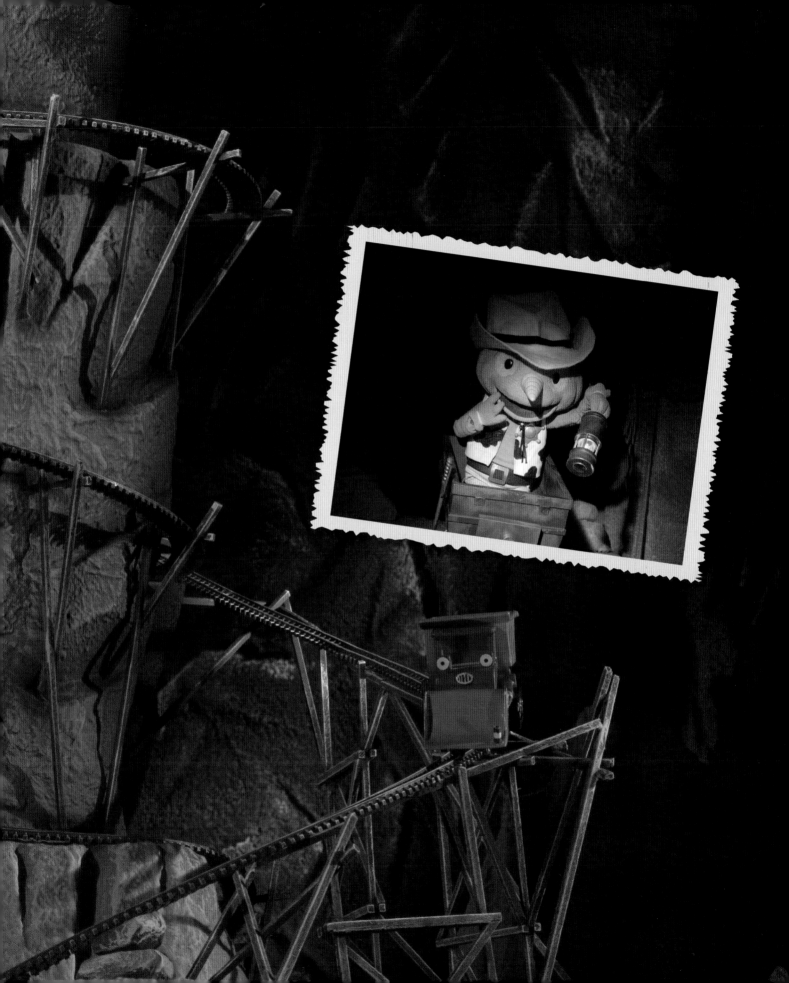

"Wow! That was brilliant – just like a roller coaster!" panted Spud.

"Just my luck," Muck said sadly. "Stuck down a gold mine, and missing out on an adventure – again!"

They spotted an arrow nailed to the wall and followed it. When they couldn't walk any further because of some fallen rocks, Muck chanted 'Built to be wild!' and bravely cleared a pathway.

But the next arrow was a complete puzzle.

"It's pointing upwards," said Spud. "That can't be right."

All of a sudden a roof timber fell, leaving a hole in the ceiling where the arrow was pointing. They used the miner's lamp to peer into the hole.

"There's something stuffed in here," said Muck, as the something hit him on the head.

"I know what that is," said Spud. "It's a saddlebag – cowboys on horseback carry their clean socks and toothbrushes around in them!"

"We could give it to Dollar, Rio's horse," said Muck, as the dusty pair walked on.

Above ground, Bob and the rest of the gang had been hammering and mixing and fixing the old buildings in Cactus Creek.

"Hot diggety dawg!" hooted Jackaroo when the saloon was finished. "This looks great, Bob! Rio, Cactus Creek is going to be better than before!"

"There's still lots left to do when you're gone," said Rio to Bob, as she turned to thank him. "But y'all have made me the happiest cowgirl in the whole of the West!"

Suddenly there was a loud clattering of hooves.

"Uh-oh," said Wendy, "looks like Brandy's escaped again."

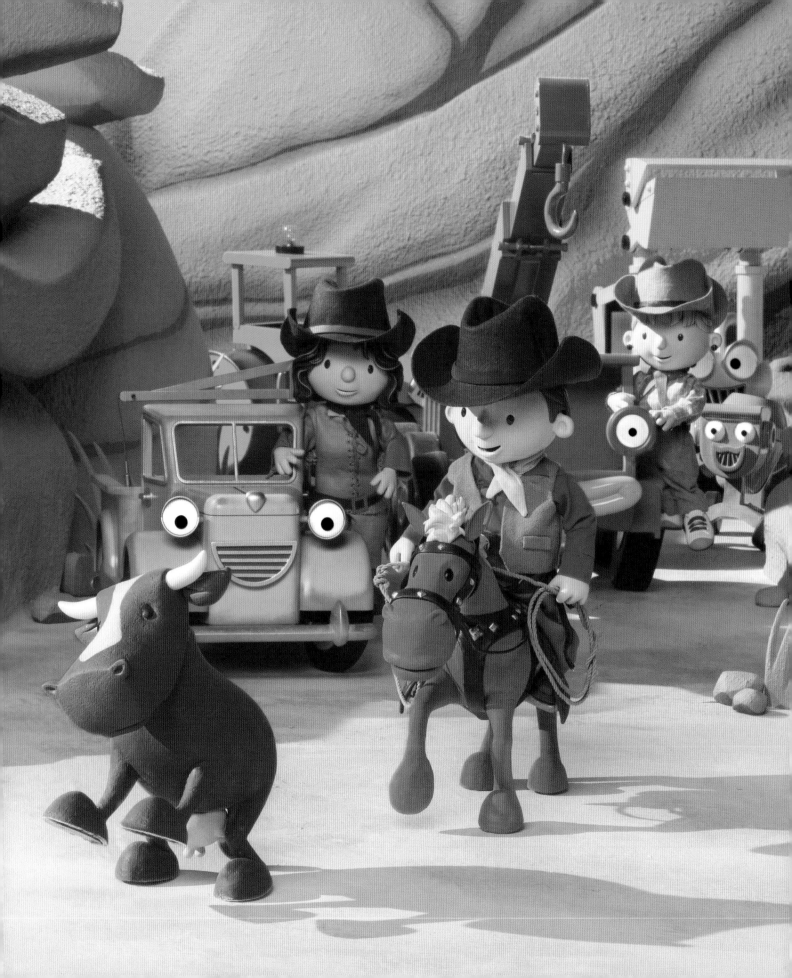

Bob leapt into Dollar's saddle and gave chase. He'd been practising hard with his lasso, and he really hoped that this time the rope would land perfectly around Brandy's neck.

"I did it!" whooped Bob, sounding surprised with himself.

"Moo!" cried Brandy, as Bob pulled her in near to the blocked off entrance of the old gold mine.

All the commotion of hooves and feet and wheels shook the ground so much that the big boulder blocking the entrance to the gold mine started to roll back into the mine.

Back inside the mine…

"Oh look, Spud! Phew!" gasped Muck. "There's a light ahead. I was beginning to think that we'd be trapped down here forever!"

It was then that they noticed the massive boulder blocking the exit.

"Oh no! Er… Muck, look!" cried Spud. "That boulder is moving - it's rolling towards us!"

Muck looked around.

"Quick – squeeze into this rock crevice, Spud!" he shouted, just as the rocked rolled over the ground where they had been standing, a few moments before.

Daylight came pouring into the dark tunnel.

"Hooray! We've made it!" cried Spud with relief. "Let's get out of here before anything else happens!"

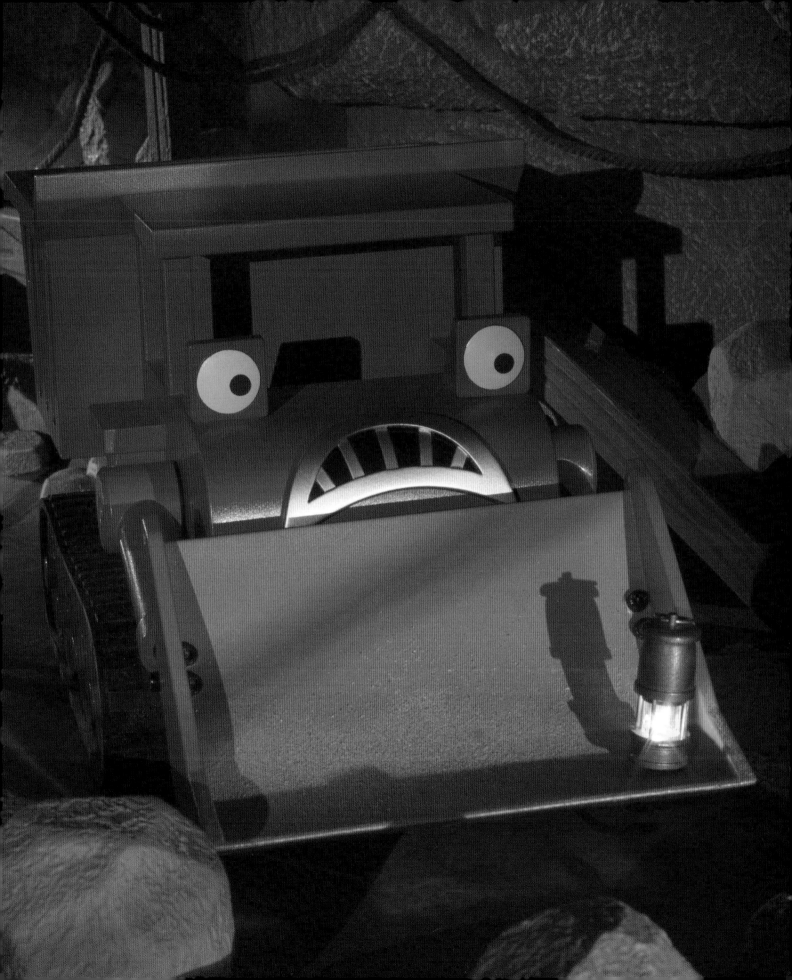

"Muck! Spud! What were you doing in there?" cried Bob, as Spud came running out of the mine, with Muck rolling behind him.

Muck began telling of their adventure in the gold mine.

"Well, in the barn there was this hole in the ground and we went on a railway track and I got hit on the head by a bag…"

"It was so dark and scary in there," added Spud. "But we were brave adventurers, weren't we Muck?"

"Well, thank goodness you are both OK," sighed Bob.

"Alrighty! You're a real cowboy adventurer now, Muck!" laughed Rio.

"Yeehah! I was built to be Wild!" shouted Muck.

Everyone laughed.

"Let's give Dollar the saddlebag, Muck," said Spud.

Muck tipped the saddlebag out
of his dumper, and Rio noticed the
double R sign on the outside.

"Ya struck gold!" whooped Rio
when she opened it. "Ya found
my great, great, Grandaddy's
stash o' gold."

"I did?" said Muck. "Wow!"

Jackaroo told Muck that he
would become a legend of
Cactus Creek.

"What – you'll tell campfire
stories about me?" Muck asked
in disbelief.

Rio nodded. "Sure, honey –
everyone's gonna wanna
hear about Lucky Muck
the adventurer!"

That evening as everyone sat down for supper, Bob smiled when he thought back to his promise about doing no building work for a week or two.

"That gold will help you return Cactus Creek to the way it was in your great, great Grandaddy's day," he said.

Rio was delighted. "Thanks a bunch, Bob and the gang... Hey! Get on yer best bib and tucker – it's time to celebrate."

Spud dressed up as Stinky Spud the most wanted scarecrow in the West, and everyone called out 'Yeehah!' as they line-danced around Rio's ranch.

"Built to be wild!" whooped Muck, the best Wild West dancer of them all.